Liam,
work hard,
be silly
be sweet, be Kind.
♡ Jordyn Koelker

What if Mummy Threw a Tantrum?

Published by Mindstir Media, LLC
45 Lafayette Rd | Suite 181| North Hampton, NH 03862 | USA
1.800.767.0531 | www.mindstirmedia.com

Printed in the United States of America
ISBN-13: 978-1-7329482-2-8
Library of Congress Control Number: 2018913451

What if Mummy Threw a Tantrum?

by Jordyn Koelker

MINDSTIR MEDIA

Miss Molly is a sweet girl,
who loves to laugh and play,
but she woke up really grumpy,
and wants everything her way.

"I want a pop for breakfast!"
She hollered at her Mummy.
Molly knows that pops aren't healthy,
but she thinks they're really yummy.

Molly's mom gave her three choices,
of healthy fruit for her to eat,
but she shook her head and crossed her arms,
and loudly stomped her feet.

She threw a wild tantrum,
Mummy's smile turned upside down,
Molly didn't like it,
when she'd see her Mummy frown.

"I'll tell you something honey,"
her mom said, "Please don't cry.
Mummy's don't throw tantrums,
And I'd like to tell you why."

I won't have time to change my clothes,
I would wear pajamas out.
but there'd be no time for play dates,
So I'd just sit at home and pout.

If Mummy threw a tantrum,
because I want to sleep in late,
We won't have time for breakfast,
And our bellies won't feel great!

What if Mummy threw a tantrum,
while we're shopping at the store?
I'd run screaming down the aisles,
then lay crying on the floor.

It would scare the other shoppers!
They'd point over to the door,
and say, "Excuse me M'am, you're being rude,
please don't come here anymore."

If Mummy threw a tantrum,
and wouldn't bathe or brush my hair,
I would be super stinky,
And I'd have tangles everywhere.

No one wants a stinky mom!
How yucky would that be?
But there's just no time for tubbies,
when I'm on a tantrum spree!

What if Mummy threw a tantrum,
and it made you kind of bitter,
when I didn't share my art supplies,
like stickers, paint and glitter?

Imagine if I wouldn't share,
your toys or anything?
I think you'd be upset,
to lose the happiness they bring.

What if Mummy threw a tantrum,
and won't buckle in the car?
I can't drive without a seatbelt,
so our van won't go too far.

We'd miss soccer and gymnastics,

and your school, the park and zoo.

You'd just hear me cry while cars passed by.

Does that sound fair to you?

Mummy really loves you
and she wants you to have fun,
But when you throw a tantrum
It affects the day for everyone.

You're the prettiest when you smile,
you smell the best when you are clean.
We get to play with lots of friends,
when we share and we're not mean.

Eating healthy gives us energy,
to run, jump, skip and hop
that's why having fruit for breakfast
is so much better than a pop.

Molly apologized to mummy,
as she climbed onto her chair.
"I'm sorry I was grumpy,"
she said, "I think I'll have a pear."